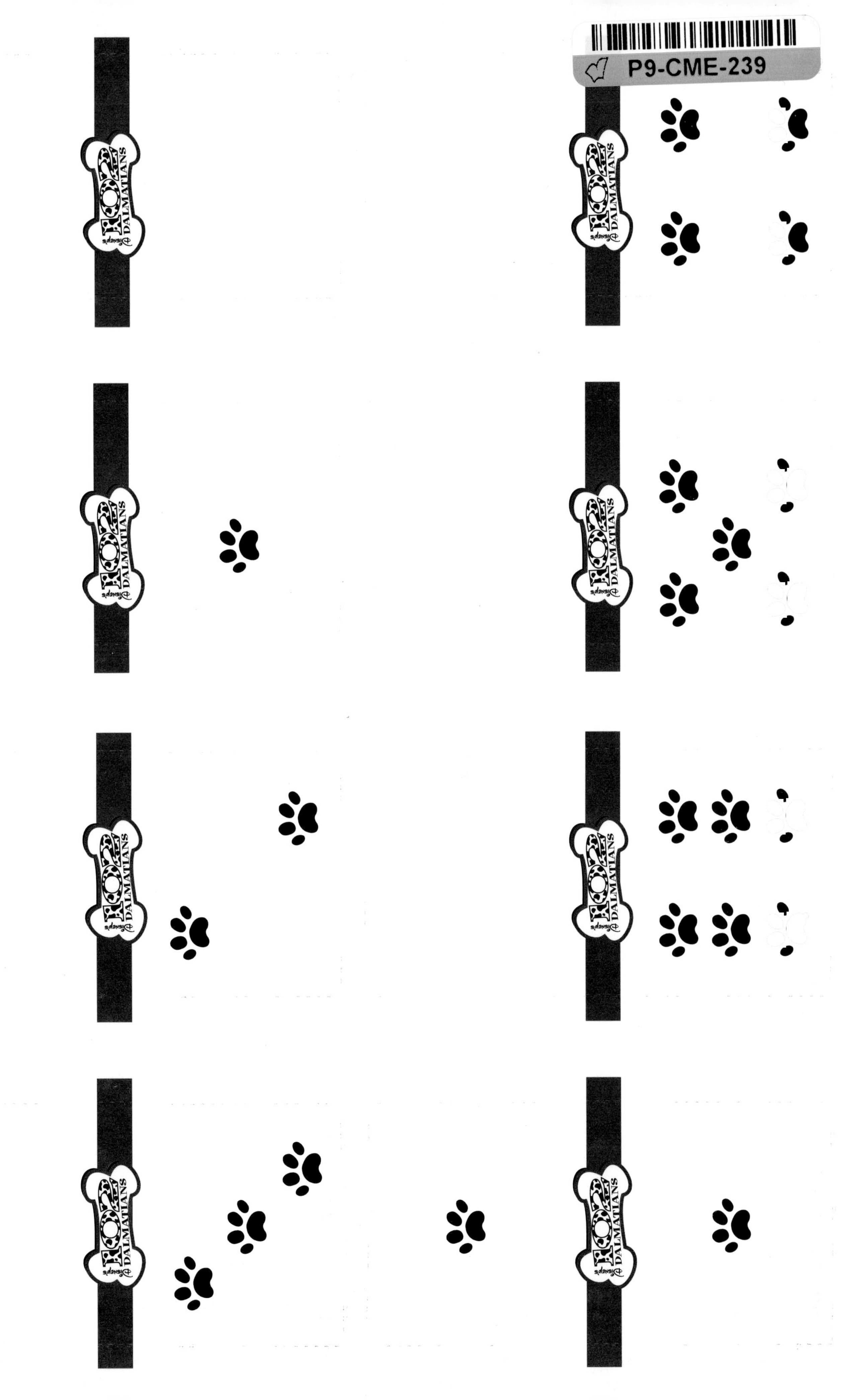
P9-CME-239
Disney's
102 DALMATIANS

Disney's
102
DALMATIANS
© Disney

Disney's
102
DALMATIANS
© Disney

Disney's
102
DALMATIANS
© Disney

Disney's
102
DALMATIANS
© Disney

Disney's
102
DALMATIANS
© Disney

Disney's
102
DALMATIANS
© Disney

Disney's
102
DALMATIANS
© Disney

Disney's
102
DALMATIANS
© Disney

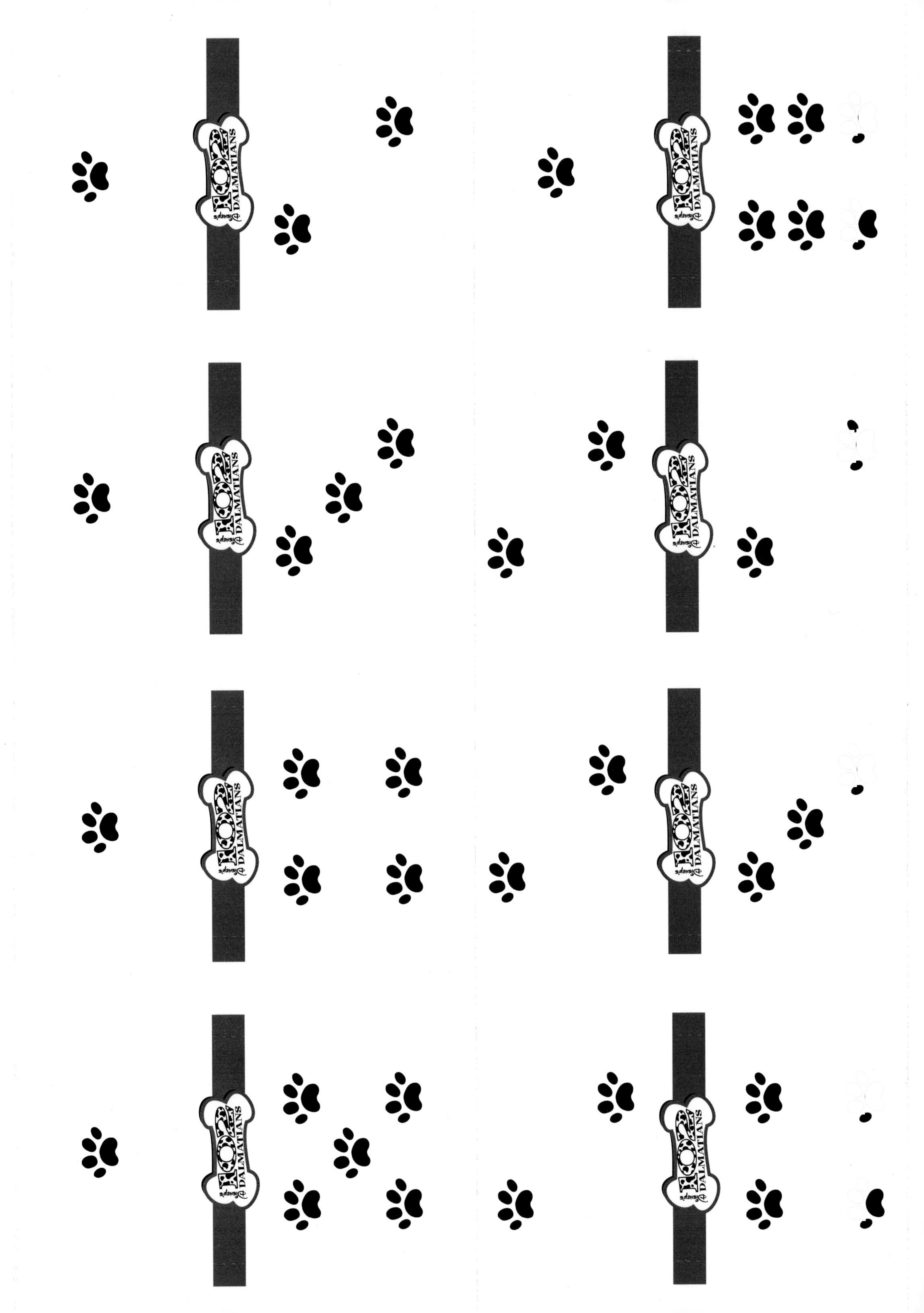

Disney's
102
DALMATIANS

Disney's
102
DALMATIANS

© Disney

Disney's
102
DALMATIANS

Disney's
102
DALMATIANS

© Disney

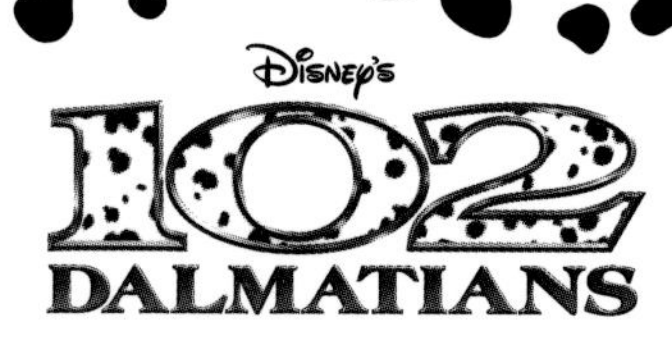
Disney's
102
DALMATIANS

Disney's
102
DALMATIANS

© Disney

Disney's
102
DALMATIANS

Disney's
102
DALMATIANS

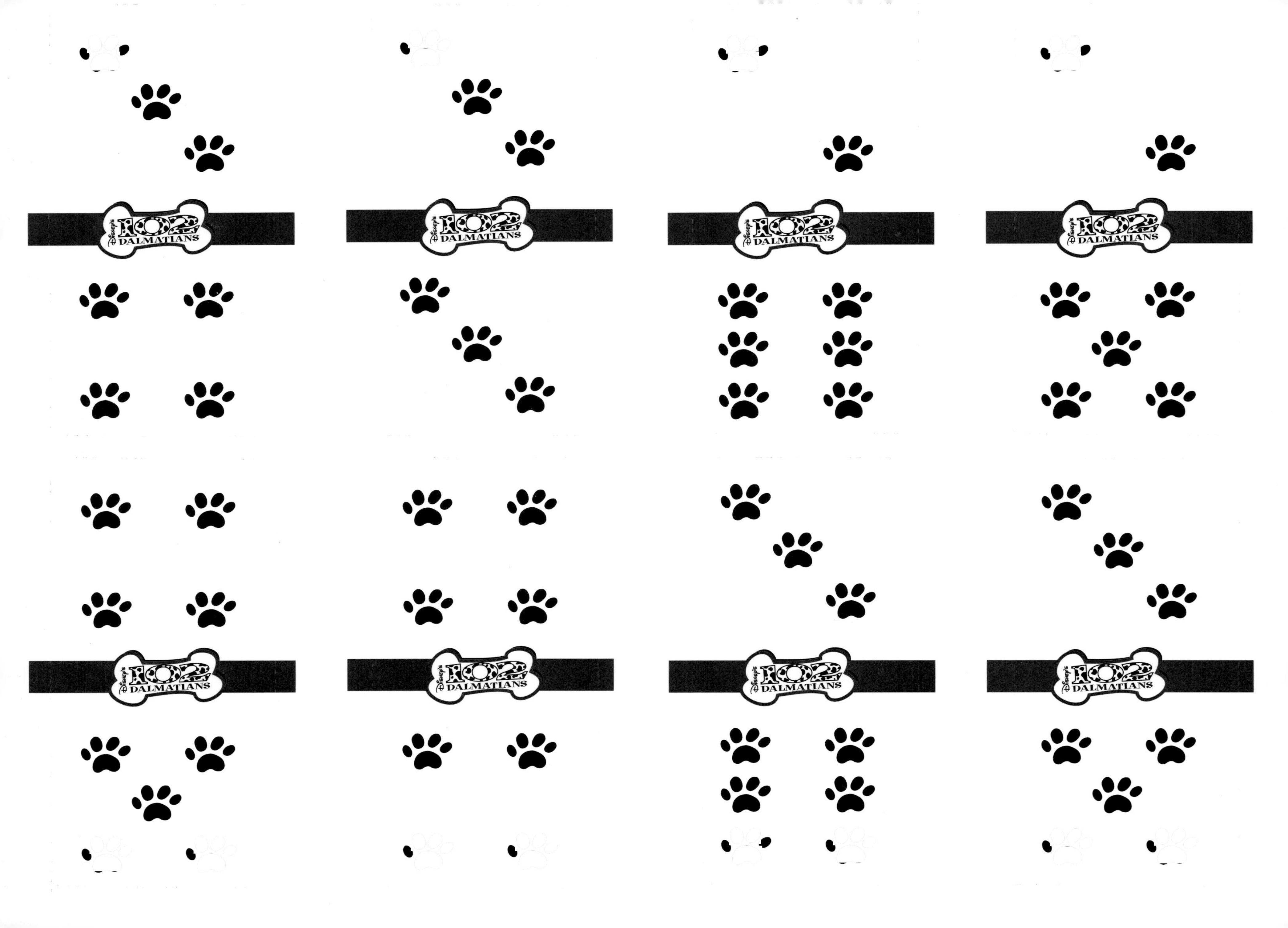
Disney's
102
DALMATIANS

Disney's
102
DALMATIANS

Disney's
102
DALMATIANS

Disney's
102
DALMATIANS

Disney's
102
DALMATIANS

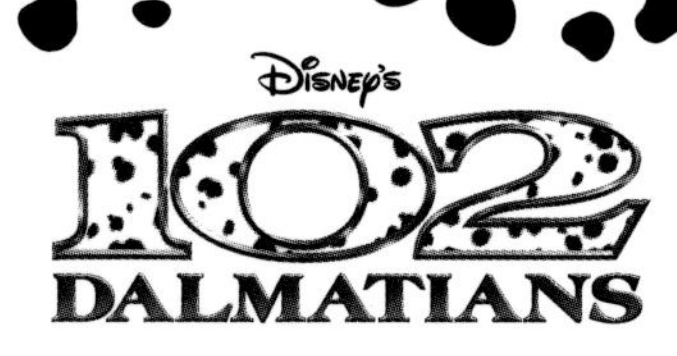
Disney's
102
DALMATIANS

Disney's
102
DALMATIANS

Disney's
102
DALMATIANS

Disney's
102
DALMATIANS

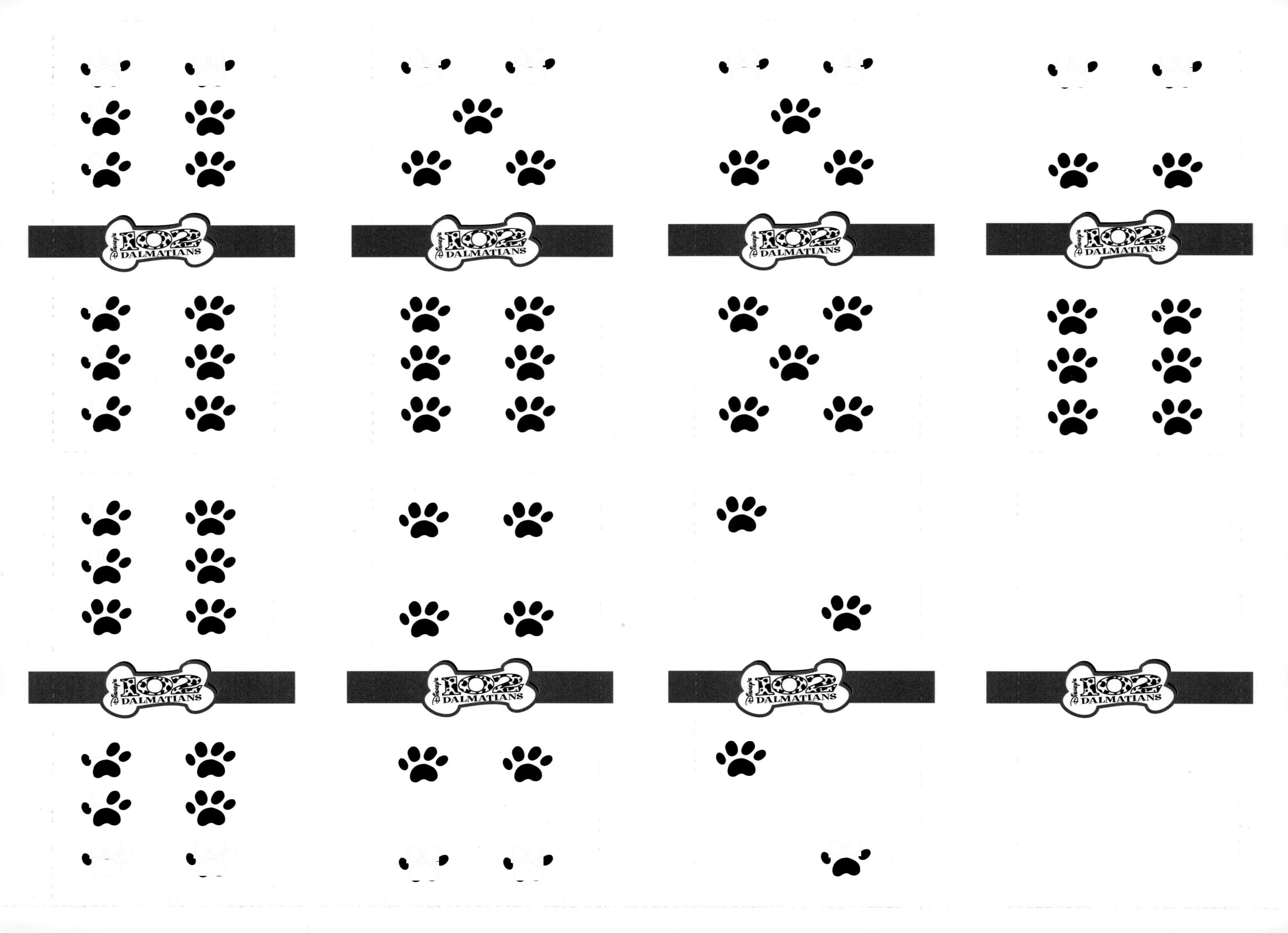
Disney's 102 DALMATIANS

Disney's
102
DALMATIANS

Disney's
102
DALMATIANS

© Disney

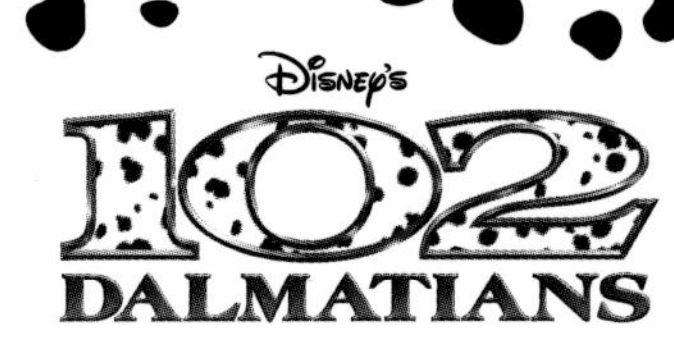

Disney's
102
DALMATIANS

© Disney

Disney's
102
DALMATIANS

© Disney

Disney's
102
DALMATIANS

© Disney

Disney's
102
DALMATIANS

© Disney

Disney's
102
DALMATIANS

© Disney

Disney's
102
DALMATIANS

© Disney

Written by Rebecca Gómez

Designed by Paul W. Banks

MOUSE WORKS™

Visit www.disneybooks.com

For information address Mouse Works, 114 Fifth Avenue, New York, New York 10011-5690.

102 Dalmatians is based on the book *The Hundred and One Dalmatians*, by Dodie Smith, published by The Viking Press.

Board game on pages 14 & 15

CONTENTS

Instructions for domino card games on pages 26–29

Cruella De Vil

"Do call me Ella, Cruella sounds so cruel!"

"Oh, Fluffy, now Mummy can start a new life."

"Hair must be a statement, a reflection of our inner life."

"I've got spots before my eyes."

"I'm back! And this time it's personal!"

Cruella's cake is cooked.

Oddball

WHY DOES CRUELLA ALWAYS ORDER BIG MEALS IN RESTAURANTS?
So she can take home a doggy bag!

DID YOU HEAR THE ONE ABOUT THE GIANT DALMATIAN?
Yes, it's quite a tail!

WHY ARE THE POLICE INTERESTED IN CRUELLA?
Because she has a spotty record!

WHY DID ODDBALL CROSS THE STREET?
To get away from Cruella!

WHAT DOES ODDBALL HAVE IN COMMON WITH AN OAK TREE?
Bark!

Woof!

WHAT'S THE BEST WAY TO KEEP A DALMATIAN PUPPY SAFE FROM CRUELLA?
Keep it from being spotted!

WHY DID ALONSO PUT THE PUPPY NEAR THE RADIATOR?
Because Cruella said she wanted a hot dog!

WHY DO YOU HAVE TO BE CAREFUL WHEN IT'S RAINING CATS AND DOGS?
So you don't step in a poodle!

WHAT'S A FAVORITE DALMATIAN PARTY GAME?
Connect-the-dots!

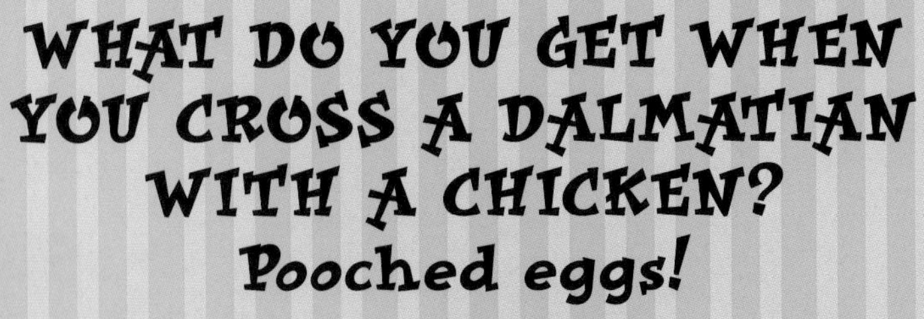

WHAT DO YOU GET WHEN YOU CROSS A DALMATIAN WITH A CHICKEN?
Pooched eggs!

puppy
power

KNOCK, KNOCK.

Who's there?

DOGGONE.

Doggone, who?

DOGGONE OUT THE DOOR!

CRUELLA:
I keep seeing spots before my eyes!

ALONSO:
Have you seen a doctor?

CRUELLA:
No, just spots!

WHAT'S WORSE THAN A SNAKE WITH A RASH?
A Dalmatian with a sore spot!

WHY DOES CHLOE LOVE THE PUPPIES SO MUCH?
Because she has a real soft spot for them!

Take a Walk

HOW CAN YOU TELL IF A DALMATIAN HAS BEEN IN YOUR REFRIGERATOR?
By the paw prints in the butter!

WHY DO DALMATIANS HAVE LONG LEGS?
So that their feet will reach the ground!

WHEN DOES A DALMATIAN HAVE A TRUNK?
When it's going on vacation!

WHAT DO DALMATIANS HAVE THAT NO OTHER DOG HAS?
Dalmatian puppies!

ith Attitu

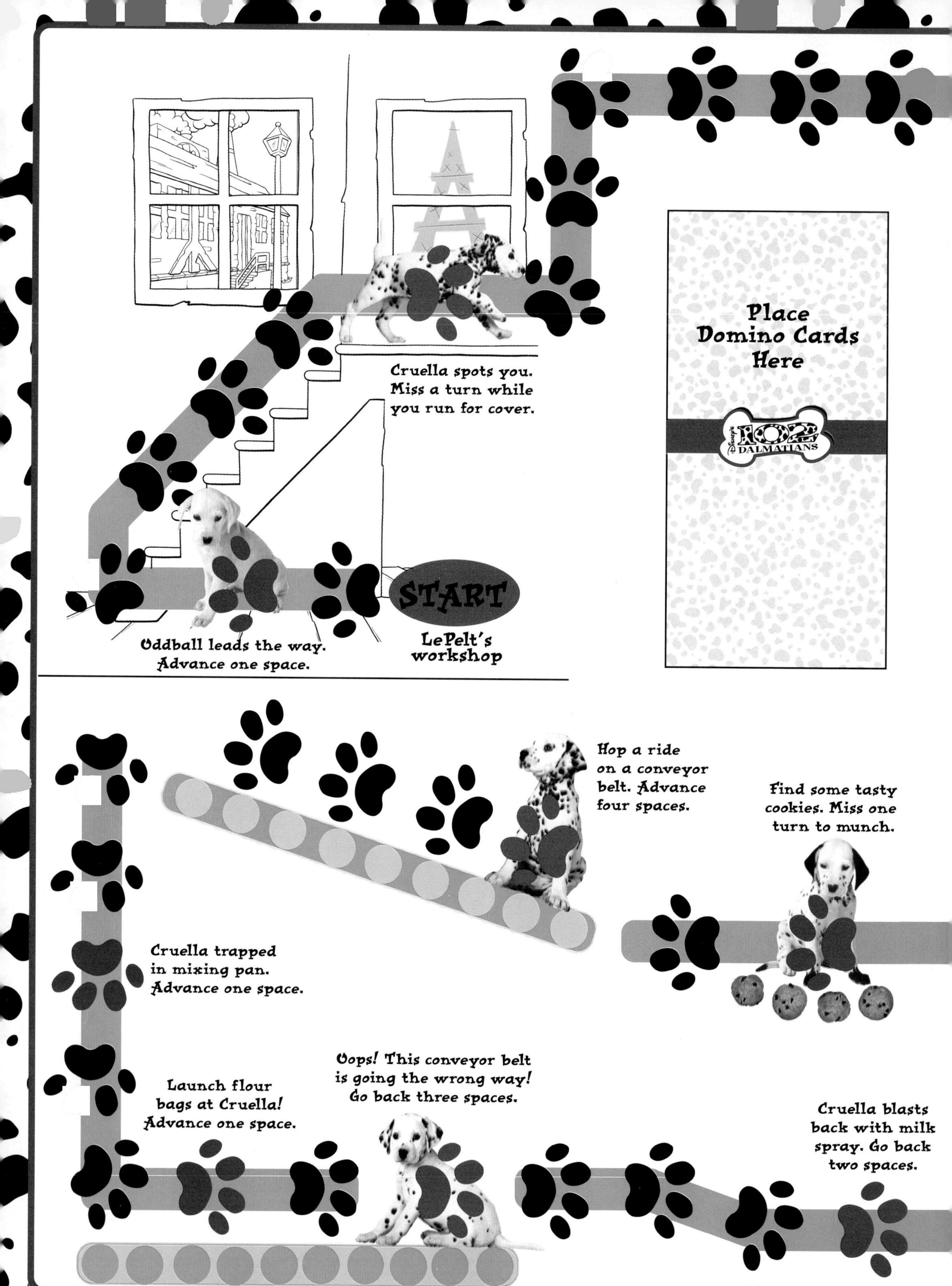
Place
Domino Cards
Here
Disney's 102 Dalmatians
Cruella spots you.
Miss a turn while
you run for cover.
START
Oddball leads the way.
Advance one space.
LePelt's
workshop
Hop a ride
on a conveyor
belt. Advance
four spaces.
Find some tasty
cookies. Miss one
turn to munch.
Cruella trapped
in mixing pan.
Advance one space.
Oops! This conveyor belt
is going the wrong way!
Go back three spaces.
Launch flour
bags at Cruella!
Advance one space.
Cruella blasts
back with milk
spray. Go back
two spaces.

Rescue the Puppies!

The object of this game is to get the Dalmatian puppies from the basement of LePelt's Paris workshop, through the bakery, and safely back to Second Chance Dog Shelter as quickly as possible. You may have as many players as you like. The winner is the first person to move his/her marker all the way to the puppies' new home!

- Find a bead, button, or coin for your marker.
- Place the game cards, face down, in the spot provided on the game board.
- Draw cards to determine who goes first. Whoever draws the card with the most paw prints goes first. Whoever gets the second-highest value goes second, and so on.
- Each player draws one card from the pile and, adding up the total number of paw prints, moves the corresponding number of spaces. Replace the card, face down, at the bottom of the pile.
- Follow other directions on game board.

Good luck, the puppies are counting on you!

You're in the bakery. Run away from Cruella. Advance one space.

Avoid fiery oven. Go back three spaces.

Cruella's cake is cooked! Advance one space.

Cruella is headed back to jail. The puppies are saved. Ruff!

Puppy Love

Second Chance Friends

Meet Waddlesworth.
He thinks he's a
rottweiler.
Waddlesworth says: "All's fair in
tug-of-war!"
"Kiss the girl!"
"Dogs can fly!"
"Move over,
Spottie."

Fluffy

"He's a hairless breed.
I thought that
appropriate, considering."

"Look,
he's smiling at me!"

WHAT IS CRUELLA'S
FAVORITE TYPE OF WEATHER?
When it's raining
cats and dogs!

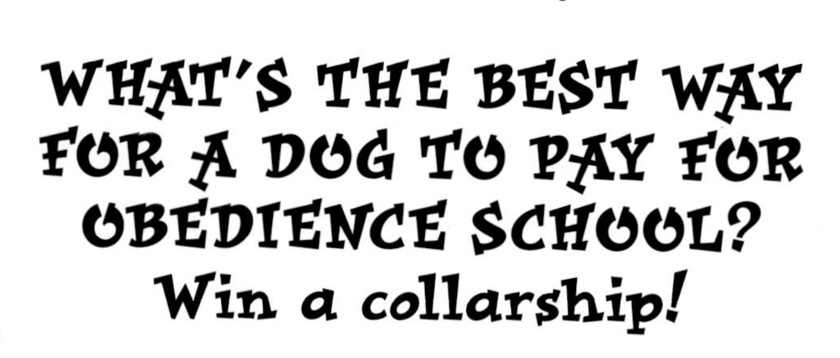

WHAT'S THE BEST WAY
FOR A DOG TO PAY FOR
OBEDIENCE SCHOOL?
Win a collarship!

Save Our Home

"All's fair in tug-of-war!"

"You and your mangy pack are out of here tomorrow!"

Digger

Drooler

Chomp

"Give us another chance."

"I don't trust anyone who knowingly puts Cruella De Vil anywhere near dogs."

"Sixteen Dalmatian puppies were reported stolen last night."

Beware Cruella

AFTER THE DALMATIAN PUPPY COAT, WHAT IS THE NEXT PIECE OF CLOTHING CRUELLA WANTS TO CREATE?
A poodle skirt!

WHAT'S BLACK AND WHITE AND RED ALL OVER?
An embarrassed Dalmatian!

WHY IS CRUELLA'S HOUSE SO MESSY?
Because she let it go to the dogs!

Cruella Cake

DOMINO'S DOMINOS

(two to four players)

Place the dominos face down. Each player (up to four) draws one domino. Whichever player draws the highest domino (add the numbers together) goes first. Each player gets seven dominos. Do not reveal your dominos to the other players. The first player puts down one domino, face up. (It's best to put down the highest number that you have, because points are added up at the end, and whoever is still holding the most, loses.) The next player must match the number at either end of the domino. If a player does not have a match, he or she must draw from the deck until a match can be made. If a player lays down a double number, he or she may make another play. The first player to play all of his or her dominos wins. If no player can use all of their dominos, then players must add up the value of the dominos in their hands and receive this number of points. The player with the fewest points wins.

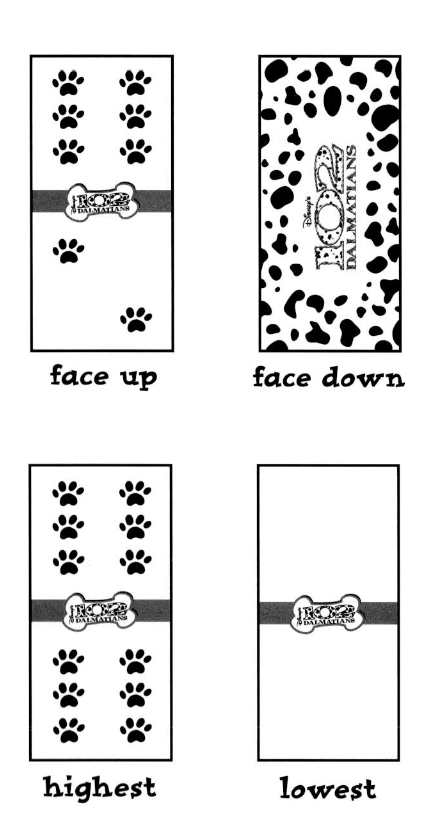

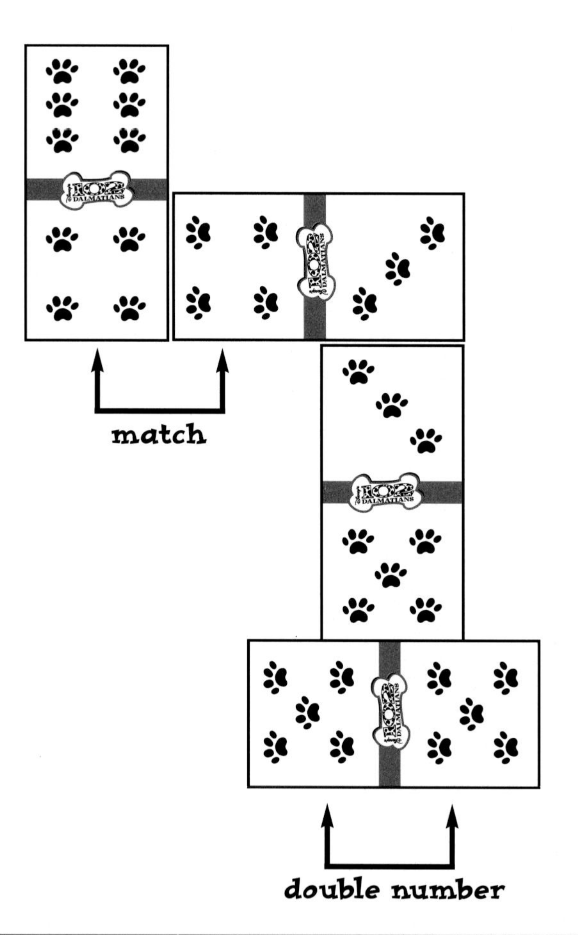

SIX PUPPIES

(two to four players)

Six Puppies is a variation of Domino's Dominos.

Instead of matching equal numbers, however, players must place dominos together whose sum equals six. For example, you can put a two next to a four, a one next to a five, etc. If a player cannot make a sum of six, he or she must draw from the deck until a six can be made. The first player to play all of his or her dominos wins. If no player can use all of their dominos, then players must add up the value of the dominos in their hands and receive this number of points. The player with the fewest points wins.

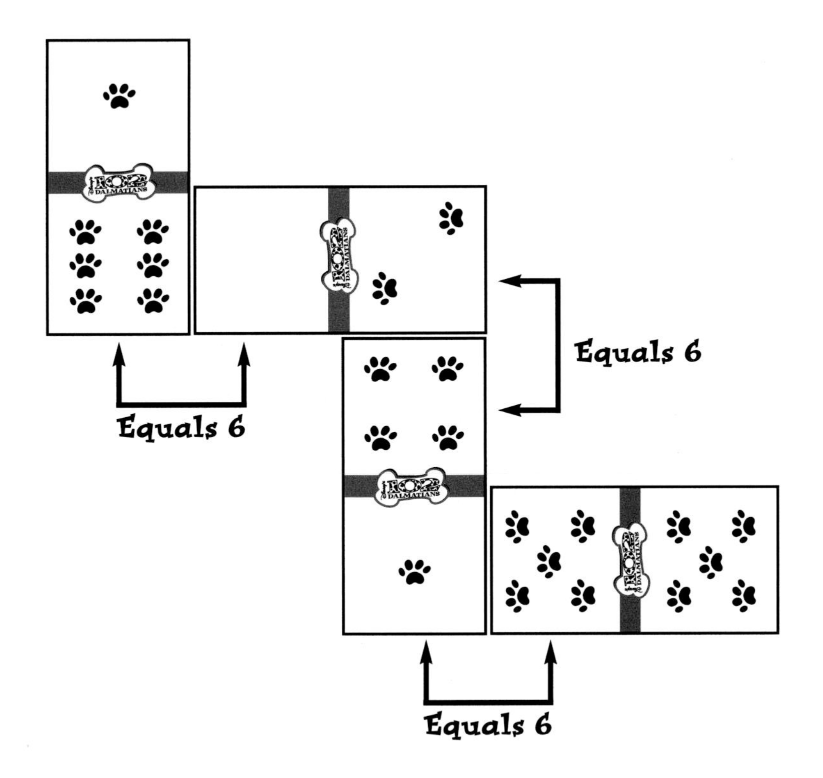

CRUELLA PLAYS ALONE
(one player)

Place all the dominos face down and shuffle them well. Arrange them all in one long row, side by side. Next, turn them all face up, leaving them in order. Starting from the left end of the row, start counting from 0 to 12, touching a domino as you say each number. Add the spots on each domino as you say the number; if the number you say matches the spots on the domino, you may remove that domino. When you reach 12, starting counting again from 0. When you reach the end of your row, close up all of the spaces and begin again from the left-hand side. The object is to remove all of the dominos.

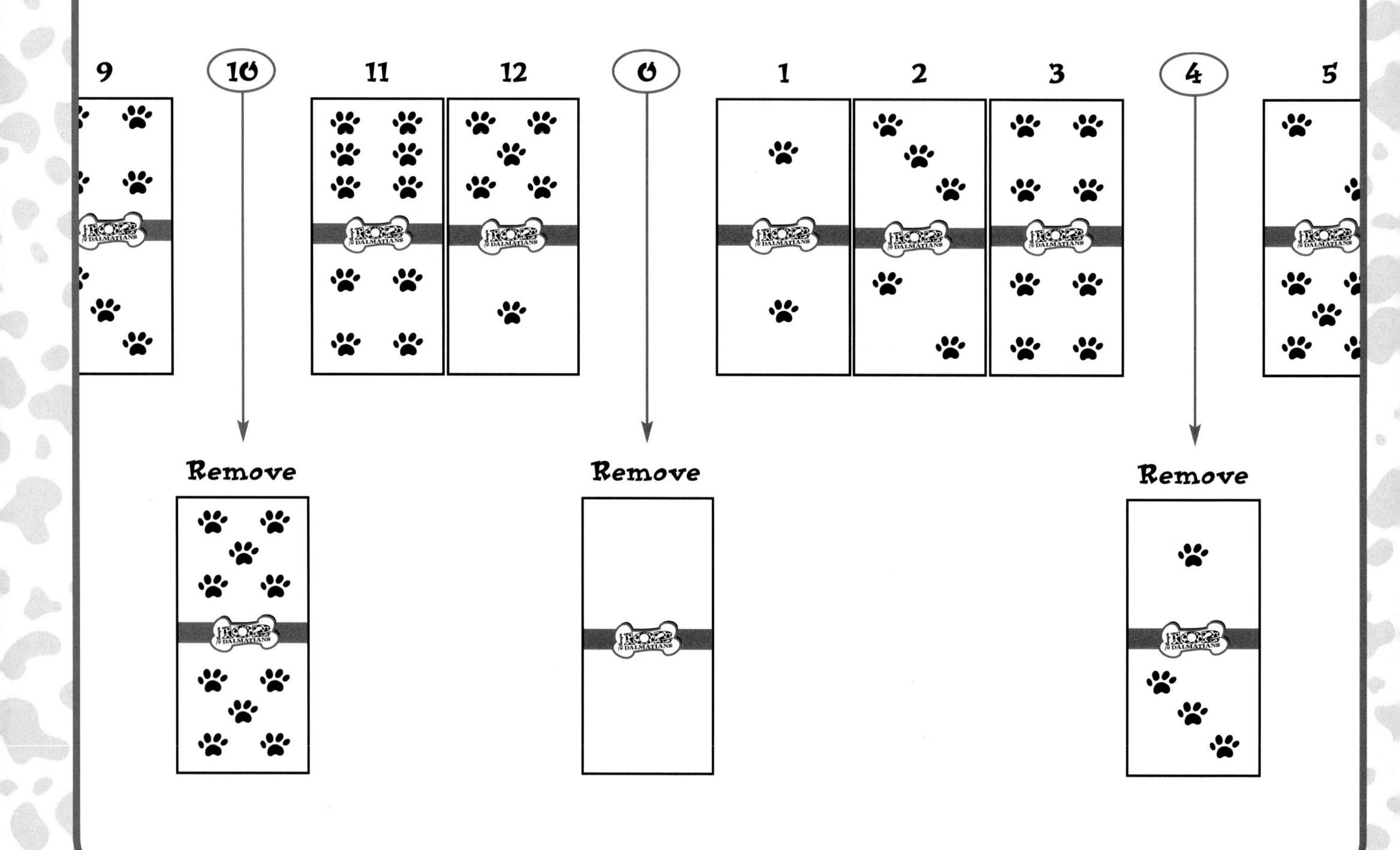

DALMATIAN CONCENTRATION

(two to four players)

After giving your cards a good shuffle, lay out three rows with six cards in each row, face down. Each player turns over two cards at each turn; if you are able to make a match, you may remove both cards to stack in pairs by your place. Fill their spots with more cards from the deck. If you make a match, you may take another turn. Keep playing until all of the cards are gone. The player with the most pairs wins.

Note: A match is made if the top or bottom paw prints of one card match the top or bottom paw prints of the other.

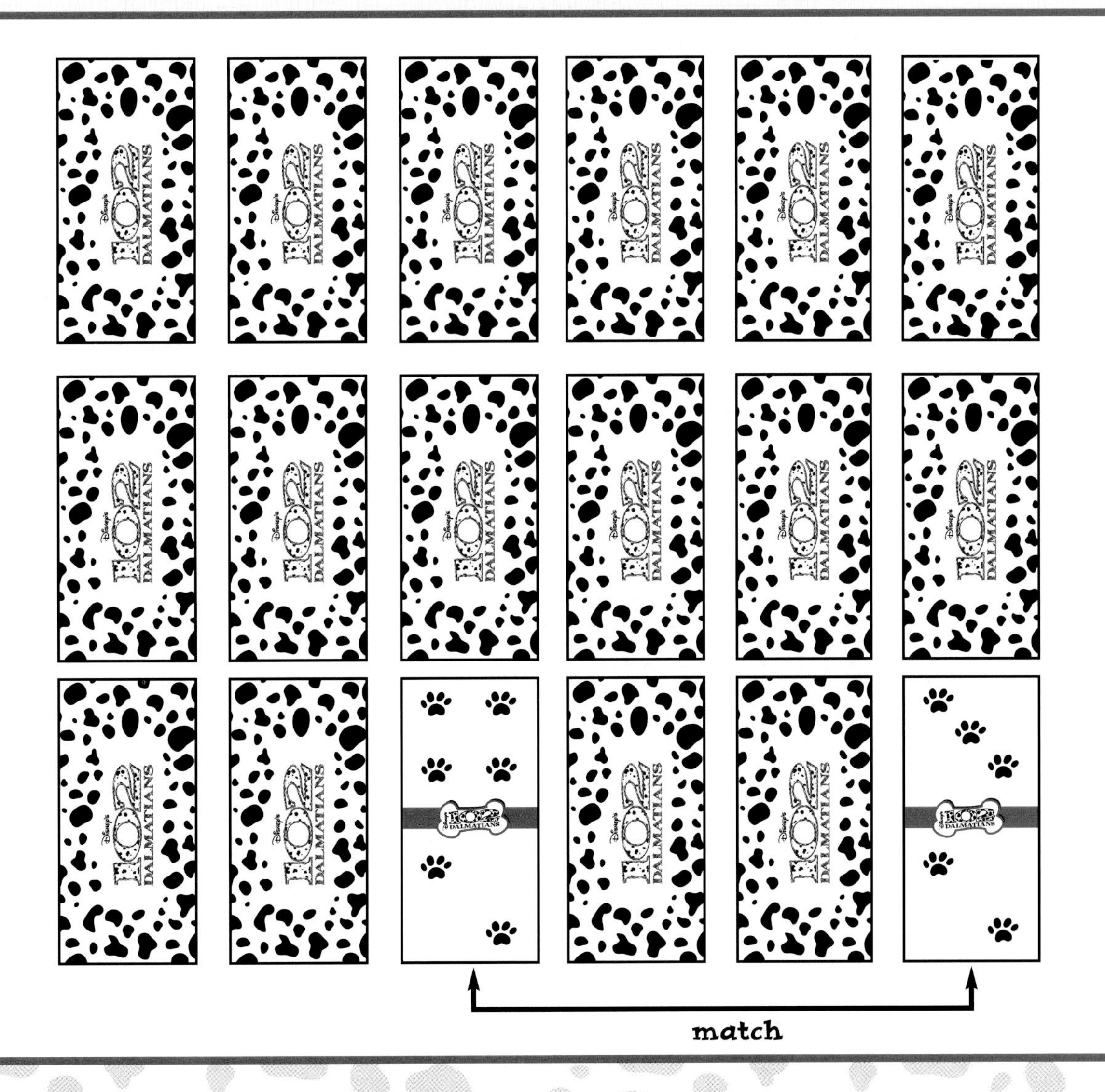

PIN THE TAG ON THE COLLAR

(two to twelve players)

To Play: Hang the puppy poster from the back cover on a wall. Cut out the tags on the opposite page. Each player chooses a tag. Then, one by one, each player is blindfolded and tries to tape his or her tag to the puppy's collar. The player who gets his tag closest to the outlined spot on the collar wins. For an extra challenge, the player can get spun around in a circle before heading for the poster!

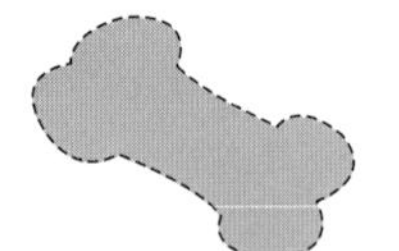

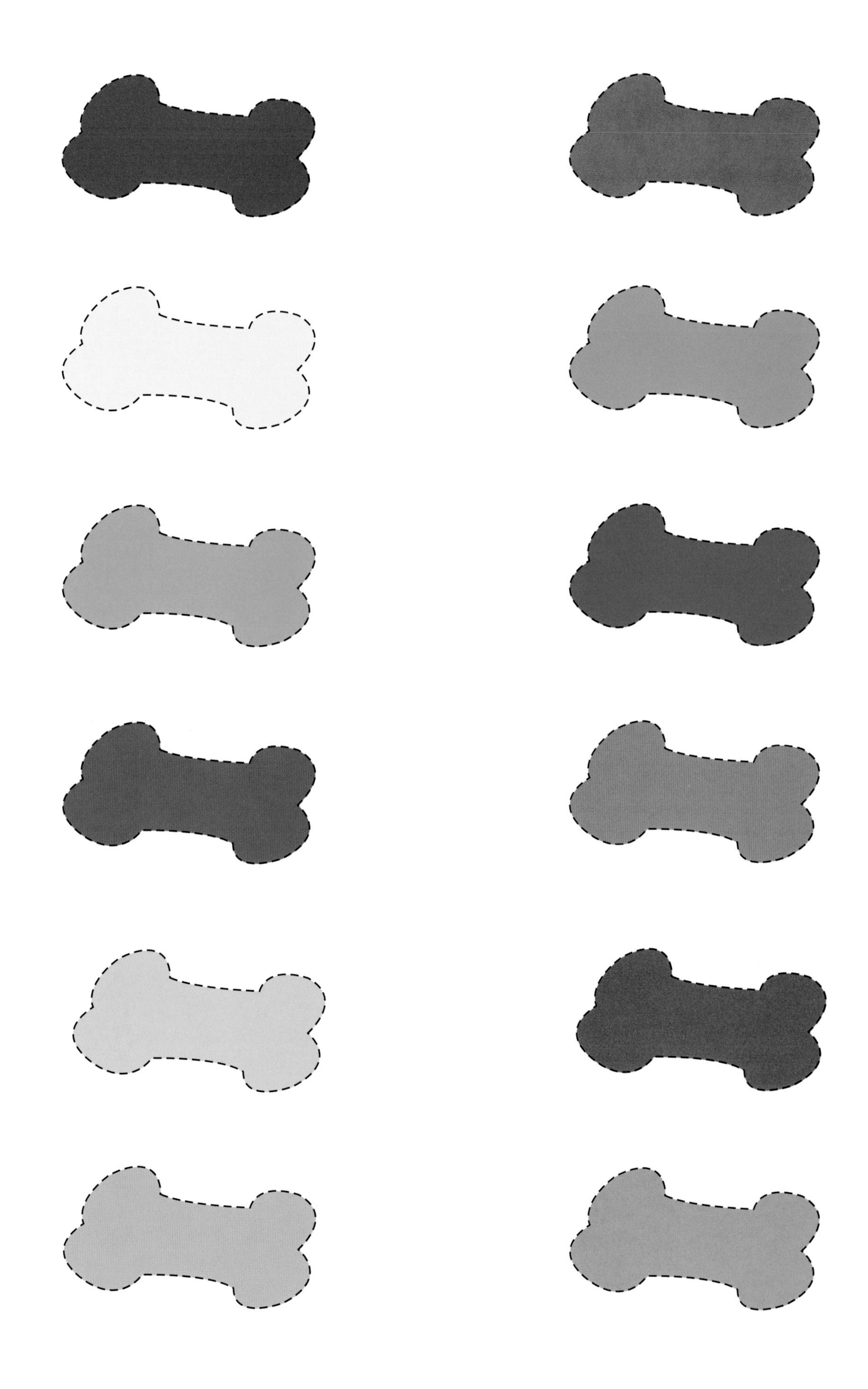

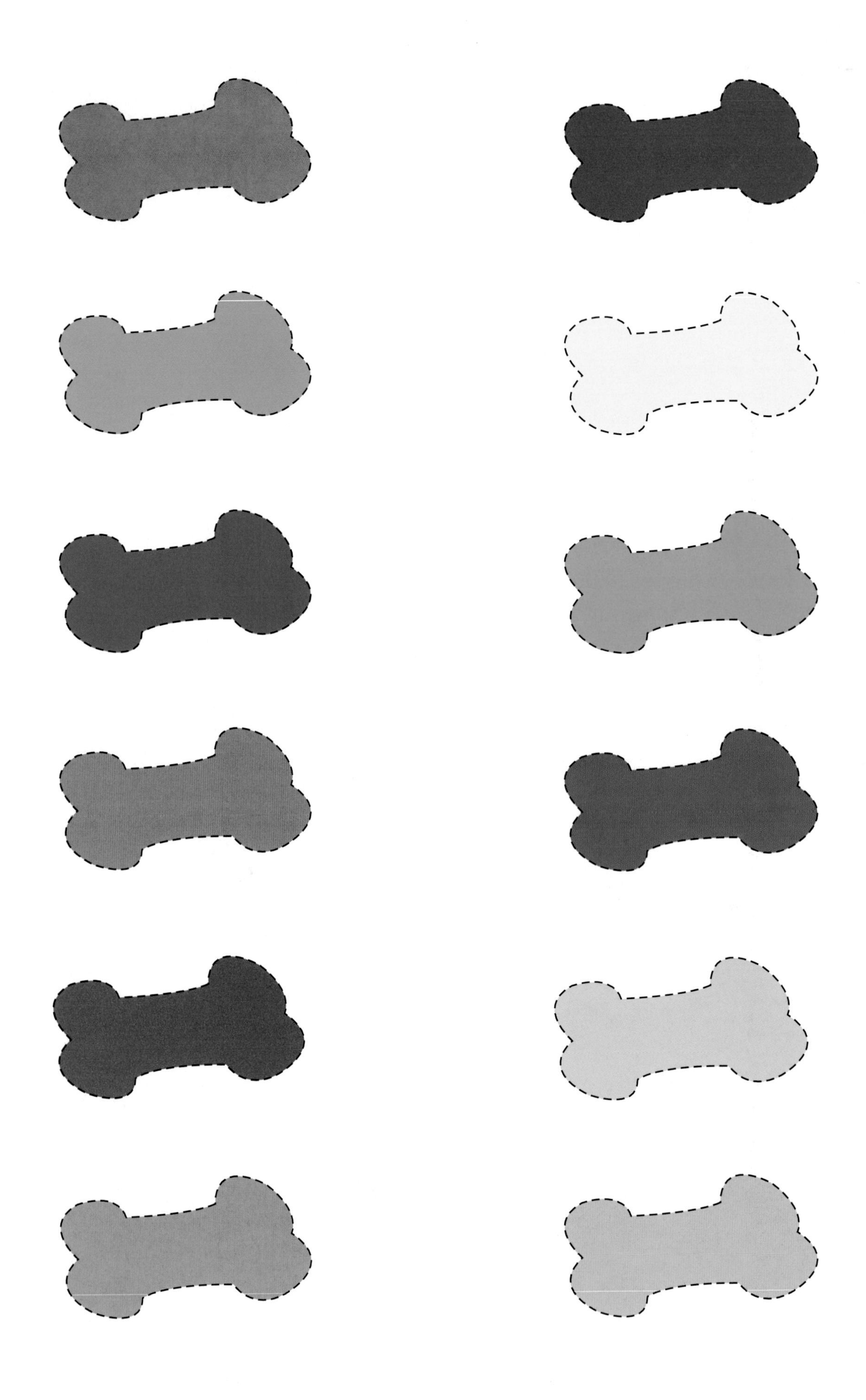